Travels with Ralphie

by
Mark Richard Arendas

ISBN: 1482669269
ISBN-13: 9781482669268
Library of Congress Control Number: 2013904610
CreateSpace Independent Publishing Platform,
North Charleston, SC

TABLE OF CONTENTS

1

THANKS TO EVERYONE

You have all inspired me to pursue this endeavor. It's been an interesting challenge. The concept is to create a short story with a serious message in a humorous fashion. I especially want to thank my daughter, Kate for noticing Ralph, and bringing him into our home. As well I would like to thank my wife Elizabeth who has stuck with me through thick and thin. Thank you also to mom and dad for being there. Barbie my twin sister has always been there as well as my sister Jennifer. The main characters are Ralphie, a four-year-old shih tzo mix, and Lou, a very successful former real estate developer. While Ralphie is a four year old canine, he is twenty four in human years. (And in many respects, much wiser and seasoned then most twenty-four year old young adults of today)

Lou is a little disheveled. He has a three-day growth, and his hair (or what's left of it) is always out of place. Handsome and tall with steel blue focused eyes, he is still an impressive figure. Lou rescues Ralphie and hires him as his personal driver. Dog drives human, not human drives dog. Ralph is very well kept. He wears his hat, gloves, and jacket.

They begin their journey in the cold mountains of rural Pennsylvania. As the relationship develops, it becomes obvious that the roles change. Who is the adult, and who is the child? Who is the mentor, and who is the mentored?

Life is full of serious situations. We are constantly being pulled in multiple directions—texting, emailing—but rarely listening to people or enjoying the simple things such as a passing cloud, a chirping bird, or a beautiful sunset. So let's just have some fun. Off we go with Ralphie and Lou. Have fun and enjoy the ride!

2

HOW WE MET

Compassion\ *kam- `pash-an*\
noun: sympathetic feeling:
pity, mercy- compassionate\ *adj*

Ralphie was a homeless, street-smart guy. A mere eight pounds with bowed legs, he was on the verge of becoming just another discarded canine casualty without a place to go or someone to take care of him. But I saw something in his eyes: he wanted to succeed and become something special.

His owner, Clara, was down and out too, and she told me to take him. Her face was weathered. Excess stress and tough times had taken its toll. We were in front of a discount store in the middle of rural Pennsylvania. I handed her fifty dollars, which she at first refused. She then reached out with her dry, overworked hands and said thank you. I never saw her again.

I looked at Ralphie, and he understood. We all need help at various points in our lives, maybe just a few extra dollars, maybe just a pat on the back and some words of encouragement. It's usually a random moment when an unknown individual reaches out to help that makes a life-long difference. This random meeting began our journey. He needed a pal and companion. I happened to be in the right place at the right time.

But Ralphie needed a little TLC. His ears were overgrown, and his eyelashes were coated with "stuff." He needed a shave (check out his picture). His teeth were a little crooked, but with some attention and care, we could fix them.

I saw that he was ready for a new chapter in his short life. Look into someone's eyes and you will know the truth. As I looked into Ralphie's eyes, I could see a glimmer of hope and trust. He was ready to begin our journey.

Even though Ralphie was just a goofy dog, he could speak English very well. I found out later that he spoke three other languages, but we can get into that at another time.

A few words about me: I was a very successful business-person. I diversified from real estate into light manufactur-ing. Luck played a part in my success, but I worked very hard. Within twenty years I had amassed a ten-million-dol-lar fortune, but I always traveled with little cash. I relied on my instincts and hard work.

Let's get on with our journey.

It was a cold, snowy night. Pennsylvania can be very challenging during the frigid months of winter. Ralphie asked if we could get a coat and hat. I explained to him I only had enough for one or the other. Priorities.

He understood. What did he pick? Of course the best coat at Wal-Mart, a macho jet fighter leather jacket with attached scarf. But I obliged. He was worth it. So we tried on a few sizes. I decided to purchase him a leather helmet too!

"Ralph, can you fly a plane?"

"Uh, no, but the local padoodle girls will love the look. Just watch me in action."

"Ralph, jump into my car. Let's begin our journey."

Lets begin our journey. He jumped up into my 1965 Ford Mustang. Lots of rust and a failing transmission.

"Ralph, we are going to do a lot better than this car. I have some fun plans in mind for the two of us."

We pulled up to a scary motel. He looked at me, and I said it was OK. It was warm, with a hot shower, and at seventy-five dollars a night, it was a great deal.

Ralph climbed into his bed and I into mine. His cell phone rang; it was some poodle from the past.

"Ralph, turn it off." I wanted to speak with him.

"Ralph, what would you like to do? Where do you want to go?"

"I don't know," Ralph said, "but it's going to be a journey. And I want you there with me."

He started to snore.

"Wake up! Let's keep talking!" I said. Sometimes communication can be tough between two humans, never mind a guy and a goofy dog.

We spoke about the future again.

"Ralph, if we are going on a journey, I want you to be my driver. We can get one of those old style limos. You are a little guy, but with a few modifications—I know just the guy—a couple times behind the wheel and you will have it down. I can ride in the back, you know, reading the *Wall Street Journal,* and you can drive."

"But you've got to sit up and look sharp. Let us go to the Numb Nutz tailor shop. He is a local shih tzo tailor. Numb makes the finest canine suits around. Numb also has a hat maker. His name is Bald Spot. It will be great, just you and I. No worries but to take a few journeys."

With that we decided to do what guys do best: a nice blasting contest before we dozed off. So Ralphie blasted one off first. It was a good one but then I let loose with a major flamethrower. Wow, I thought the room was going to ignite.

He was really ticked off and accused me of rigging the competition. I guess the burrito special bag discarded on the floor was enough evidence.

"OK Ralph and you fine dined on a can of Country Stew for dogs. I think we competed on equal grounds. Let's call it a draw. Competition will continue at some future date. Let's start off nice and fresh tomorrow. Good night, Ralph."

"Good night, Lou. See you in the morning."

With that, we dozed off.

3

THE EARLY DAYS

Companion \ *kam-pan-yan*\ *n [Of compagon,*
fr LL companion, companion, lit ,one who shares bread.
Fr,L. com- together + panis bread] **1.** *An intimate friend or*
associate: Comrade **2.** *One of a pair of matching things.*

"**R**alph, time to rise! Ralph, time to rise! RALPHIE BOY, TIME TO RISE!"
We all know the look. Turn over and ignore. Time for more sleepy time. OK, fine. I'll give him a few more zzzzzzzzzzzzzees. I rolled over, fired off few more good blasts. Ahh, it was wonderful! Wafting from under the sheets, it was paradise!

"OK, enough of the ten-year-old humor; let's get on the road."

He still wouldn't budge. I showered my slightly stinky, overweight body and returned to the sack.

"Hey Ralph! Ralphie!" I called.

9

"Yeah, what's up?" he asked.

"Please talk to me about your life story. Where did you begin your discovery of America?"

"Communist China" he replied.

"We ended our journey in Bethlehem." Ralph concluded.

"You journeyed all that way from the Middle East?" I was impressed.

He just slowly shook his head and rolled his eyes.

"No, Bethlehem, PA," he said.

He was kind of incredulous. He must have been wondering; what am I getting involved with? Lou is not the sharpest tool in the box. But there is something about him, a certain unique enduring quality. Time will tell."

Ralph continued: "I came from an abandoned home. My parents had issues, but they meant well. But once the steel mills shut down, their jobs were gone. The silence was deafening. The furnaces were silent; the raw iron no longer poured from the huge, hot containers. The workers no longer walked in, thousands at a time. They would walk from South Bethlehem, cigarette in one hand, lunch pail in the other. My parents often muttered things around the dinner table about mismanagement and corrupt union guys. They both played a role in this once-thriving business."

"Did you know," Ralph asked, "the Ajax Steel Co. actually supplied the steel for the Empire State Building? They were proud mutts, but down and out. Mom was a gorgeous, bright white Lhasa Apso. Dad was a native shih tzo."

Ralph was actually born in the small river town of Nanjing, located on the Yangtze River. It was a beautiful area, home to the beginning of the Three River Gorges region.

Spectacular limestone cliffs surrounded their village. As daylight arrived the gorge would slowly change. The morning sun would ignite millions of moisture beads. They would sparkle like lights on a Christmas tree. There was also a wonderful scent in the air. It was subtle but distinct, kind of a mixture of dew and spice—mix some water, rosemary, and chive with a touch of cinnamon.

It was beautiful. Ancient villages dotted the riverbanks. These indigenous pups had lived there for centuries. But it was a dangerous area to live in. Flooding was a persistent problem.

The villagers heard lots of rumors about a huge hydroelectric dam that might be constructed to the west. It would be called the Three-River Gorges Dam Project. There would be many benefits. Electricity would be supplied to a growing Chinese population. There would be flood control for those who lived downstream.

But there was a downside too. Many millions of pups that had lived, fished, and existed in the area would be displaced. All would be moved to big cities or relocated in small, nondescript towns built above the flood line.

Would the government investment pay dividends? Time would tell.

Ralph learned Mandarin as a young lad. It was a tough upbringing. There were no grocery shops. The family relied on the river for food and income—they were fisher dogs. But the time had come; the writing was on the wall. Little dog families from everywhere were being crucified. Little dog rights were nonexistent, and it was getting worse. The Communist Party was not exactly canine friendly.

Mom and Dad scooped Ralphie Boy up, and they made their move. Time to go, Ralphie. Off to the land of opportunity and freedom. They boarded their Chinese Junk fishing boat and headed east toward Shanghai.

Ralphie described the trip as treacherous. He was the designated scout. Now, he was only eight inches tall, which challenged his view over the bow, and evil lurked around every corner. But they knew Ralph could do the job and told him so. In order to avoid predators, they traveled at night, just the three of them, slowly maneuvering in their junk, a little lantern to help them light the way. Progress was slow, but they moved with the current. They had a mission and were going to achieve it, or so they hoped. When danger appeared they ducked into a hidden cove.

Food was not an issue. Mom and Dad could provide plenty of yummy fish. (Yes, Ralph said, doggies like fish too, especially a good plate of sushi)

13

"But this was not a sushi trip," Ralphie said.

"It was a trip for survival. The journey would lead to a better life. We would be free. We would have liberty and dignity. We would live a better life. There were many hurdles to overcome. My parents were wonderful. Even during our darkest nights, they encouraged me. We could and would succeed. I believed and trusted them. Isn't that like you and me?" he asked, glancing at me from the corner of his mischievous eyes.

I nodded yes. Could I meet his expectations? The bar was set high. But we were BECOMING COMPANIONS. It was a process that would take time. We both understood the idea. I would encourage him, and he would do the same for me.

"So then what happened, Ralph?" I asked.

Ralph replied: "Enough of this for now. We can resume this conversation tomorrow. It's time to leave this fleabag hotel and purchase a suit for me. I would like to shower and need your assistance. I'm just a ten inch tall dog. Please, when I yell for you, hand me the soap. And don't look! I have a few other requests: a nice professional shave and massage."

"No problem, Ralph."

The water was turned on. Ralph had a great shower, and we were ready to move on.

"Ralphie, let's just hail a cab for now."

We sold the Mustang for nine hundred and fifty dollars. It was time to move in a different direction.

"OK, let's go."

The first stop was for a shave and a massage. It was a small boutique-type of business. I sent him in and waited in the cab. The driver's name was Habib. We had a great time talking while Ralph was getting cleaned up. Habib was from Pakistan and had worked hard to make the trip to America. There were lots of hurdles and obstacles. But he endured. Habib was earning enough to help support his family. His wife was a domestic worker. He said that between the two of these loving people, they would make it through. I believed him. He had a companion, and they believed in each other.

With that Ralph sprang out from the spa. He looked really HAPPY (guys, you know that look). His shave was a little rough, but what the heck. Ralph was a satisfied customer and ready to move on.

"Ralphie boy, I think you need a sharp new crisp suit. As my driver, a professional look is mandatory."

With that, we left the spa. Ralphie was very relaxed. He had a sort of a blissful look on his face.

"Ralph," I said, "you look real calm. How do you feel, buddy boy?"

"Good, real good," he answered.
His big brown eyes rolled back into his head.
"Ahh, it's time to find me a suit."
With that we took off.
"HABIB! Wake up!" I shouted. Our driver had fallen asleep.
"Take us to the best tailor in town! My companion needs a suit and hat! Let's GO!"
We arrived and were greeted by Wing Ding. It was the Wing Dingtailorshop in Ding Wing, Pennsylvania. Perfect.
Wing Ding was another shih tzo and had grown up in the same town as Ralphie. His wife, Ding Bat, was the actual tailor. She grew up in Bat Ding, just a mile or so from her

15

husband. This was a match made in heaven. Ralphie, Wing Ding, and Ding Bat would get along wonderfully They all spoke Mandarin. I was confident that their attention to detail and quality of workmanship would serve Ralphie well.

I stayed with Habib. He was such a hard worker that an occasional shower was probably not a top priority. The "Appleseed Air Freshinor" had expired. I opened the window a slight bit and we were fine.

But then Ralphie walked out. Shave, massage, and now a new suit and cap. I was impressed. Wing Ding and Ding Bat had done a great job. Ralph looked great. He was dressed in a sharp suit and shirt, black leather shoes and wool cap. Silk tie and cuff links too! The package was complete.

He climbed in, and we high fived. Oh yeah, we were on our way.

"HABIB," I shouted, "take us to Ajax Limo and Restoration. We need a car of our own. It's time to get busy!"

Ajax was the best operation in town. If they didn't have it, they would find it. If they couldn't find it, they would build it. I had a vision: a beautiful, shiny black limo. Not a conventional "Town Car" limo but something unique. I wanted a 1940 Caddy style.

We were lucky. A 1940 model was raised on cinder blocks. She was covered with a tarp but sat proudly at the rear of his lot. She needed work. You know, like a fifty-plus actress trying to pull her face tighter. Raise the flattened chest area, puff up the lips.

Vito the proprietor emerged.

"Vito, let's bring her back to life."

Fortunately, money was not an issue. She would look better then when she rolled off the assembly line.

Vito told me some about her history. She had one owner, a wealthy real estate developer from northeast Pennsylvania. He had amassed a huge fortune. Things changed, and he sold everything. His prize Caddy went too. So Ralphie Boy and I would take good care of her.

We couldn't wait for her facelift. But in the meantime, we had a few weeks to kill, and we decided to take a few trips. So off we went.

Ralphie loved it. We journeyed from here to there and had lots of fun. Then we returned to Vito's. The limo was perfect: super-glossy black paint, gleaming chrome bumpers, and accessories. I ran my hand over her body. It was smooth—like the top of my head, just like a baby's behind.

Ralphie opened the rear door. "Hey," he said, "let's look at your new office."

That's what we named the back sitting area: my office. It had new leather seats, a reading light, and a small bar. Vito had already stocked it with some Dom Pérignon, Cognac, and some water. We also had a small supply of lemons and limes. And the fragrance—Ahh. Nothing like new Corinthian leather.

I climbed in. It was like sitting on an exquisite living room couch. The only detail missing was a pipe rack.

"No," Vito said, "slide that door open."

There it was—my pipe rack and tobacco canister. All I had to do was supply it with some goods—some great, aromatic tobacco. Yum yum. My pipes were gone, but we could find some new ones. But they needed to be different, maybe a few carved ones. We would locate them.

The trunk had so much room. Three mature, travel worn leather pieces. Two bags for me and one for Ralphie would fit perfectly with room to spare. We need an umbrella or two. Plenty of room for all we need.

I paid Vito, and we were ready to go.

"What now?" said Ralph.

"Let's just take her for a test ride."

Ralph walked around the side of our new ride. He opened my door first and guided me in. I felt like quite the gentleman. He jumped into the cockpit. Vito had engineered Ralph's seat perfectly. Ralphie could reach the controls. His legs were short, but Vito had integrated a few extensions—kind of like small blocks on a kid's new bike.

Ralphie needed a little time to get used to driving the limo. He had driven smaller less complicated cars, ones with automatic transmissions, ones with shorter engine hoods. And then there was the four-gear transmission, he needed to shift and still see over the windshield. Well, Vito never thought about that one. So we had to develop a little retrofit. It really was simple. We found a little high chair seat booster. You know, the kind of booster that your local waitress would pull out for little snot nose Johnny at the local restaurant. But we built the seat into the existing one. It looked and worked great. Corinthian leather with a couple of arm rests.

We needed a name for our new ride.

"Ahh," Ralphie said, "the Loumobile."

"Sounds great, Ralphie boy."

I could just hear it: "Ralphie, GET THE LOUMOBILE! Immediately!"

"So where to, Lou?" Ralph asked.

"Let's head to Allentown. I've got a couple of ideas."

19

And with that command, we were off—Ralphie, our new ride, and me. What else does a guy need? Simple as that. Like the cat in the hat.

4

THE MIDDLE DAYS

Mentor- \ *men-tor*\ *noun* :
a trusted counselor or guide; also: Tutor, Coach.

"**R**alph, we need to find a pipe shop. Pipe smoking helps me think. Fine tobacco, a smooth pipe, some cognac, and we can talk some more."

Just outside of town, we found the perfect shop: Smelly's Pipe and Tobacco Co. Ralphie and I pulled up. Very impressive, I thought. Nice, big, black Caddy. Just the two of us. Ralph opened the door and helped me exit. We walked in.

The proprietor did a double take. "Yes, can I help you?" He looked at Ralph and then at me. A dog chauffeur guiding his customer in. What is this? I'm sure he thought.

The aroma was fabulous. A blend of different tobaccos AND classic pipes on the rack. They were all hand carved. I was sure we would find something special.

Sun was the proprietor. His wife Lee was second in command. They spoke in Mandarin, and a wonderful conversation ensued. They had grown up in the same city as Ralph's parents and emigrated from China. Ralph's eyes lit up. He bonded with them. They were no longer strangers, but comrades. Both parties were exchanging stories.

Sun displayed a few pipes. No doubt the hand-carved mahogany pipe from Cuba was going to be my choice. So while they conversed, I sampled the tobacco. He had dozens—one whiff here, and one whiff there. Ahh, the aroma. One tobacco was from Kentucky, one from North Carolina, one from Virginia. There were some exotic ones too. Some tobacco was from Asia, some even from Africa.

I settled on the Appleseed blend from Virginia. I was ready to complete the transaction, but Ralphie was engaged. I stepped back. His eyes were wide open. So what were they talking about? Why was Ralph so engaged? They went on and on. Mandarin can be a hard language to listen to. Without understanding, without any clue, I needed to know.

"Ralph, are we ready to go?"

"Yes."

With that, I paid Sun and Lee. Ralph walked out with me. He seemed disturbed. He opened the door, and I climbed in with a new pipe, fresh tobacco, and a new story to tell.

"Some cognac, please!" I poured one mini glass. I lit my new pipe with fresh tobacco. This was the ultimate freedom. Just me, Ralphie, and a nice mini glass of cognac. My tummy was gurgling. It must have been the bad bologna sandwich. Ahh, I blew off a few good blasts, Cahh boom, cahh boom. Just too much firepower.

Ralphie retaliated. Rat a tatt tat, ratt a tatt tat. A mild but fair shot back.

Ahh, but it was fun. We opened the windows. They were the manual crank down type so it took a few seconds. Now it was Ralphie and I.

But the multiple blasts had blown the whitewalls off the rims. We had the Loumobile towed in and repaired. We came to an agreement: cease all blasting without pulling over and exiting the Loumobile.

"Ralph, tell me about your conversation with Sun and Lee. Let's take a trip and chitchat a bit. Drive to Route 78 east. I'll let you know when to stop."

Route 78 goes east-west between New York City and western Pennsylvania. It's a wonderful road, well maintained and direct. It would be perfect for the Loumobile. We took off, and within seconds we were cruising at 80 mph on our way east.

I lit my pipe and sat back. The caddy was smooth, the shifting perfect. The Loumobile absorbed every bump with ease. It was like riding on a silky scarf. The sun had set, and the weather was changing—just a light mist. Ralph turned the wipers on. Swish, swoosh, swish swoosh. It was very relaxing—the wiper rhythm, my pipe, and a little cognac. I looked out the window. The beads of water glistened on the glass. It added a touch of beauty to our ride. I settled deeper into my seat.

"So Ralph, let's rejoin your journey to America. And please talk about your conversation with Sun and Lee."

"Sure, Chief," he replied.
"DON'T call me Chief!"
"Sure, Lou."

He continued with his story.

"Once we reached Shanghai, things started to fall apart. We were supposed to hook up with a smuggler. Our meeting place was established. We pulled our junk into a nondescript slip. Our connection's name was Whee. Whee was not there. Lee asked someone one the dock. 'Do you know Whee?'

"'Yes, but he is gone. But I will help you.'

"'And your name, please?'

"'My name is Woo.'

"'Who?'

"'Woo.'

"'Woo, what guarantee can you give us for safe travel to the US?'

"'Not much, but I will try. I can say that sometime, some day, I hope someone will do the same for me."

"We placed our faith in Woo. He guided us through the bowels of Shanghai. Everyone wanted something. Purchase a pigtail, please. Purchase an ox foot, please. They shouted in Mandarin. It's a harsh-sounding language, Lou. Not one that would appeal to you. We had nothing, and Woo continued to guide us through the maze. We just needed to get continue on our way. My dad guided us into a small port just south of Shanghai. It was teeming with activity. Handcarts were being pulled to various nooks and crannies. Goods on carts, goods on the backs of hardworking, simple people. They were just simple people, working to supply their families with the basics of life, adequate heat, a roof over their head. They couldn't rely on the corrupt government, Lou. It was up to them and they knew it. Rickshaws were everywhere, almost colliding at every turn. But they maneuvered and always avoided the collision. They didn't need stop lights or go slow signs. It was instinctive. Veer left, veer right."

"We were led to a cargo ship. It was full of various goods from China."

"'You need to go now,' Woo said. 'NOW! Get in.'

24

"We climbed the gangplank. No one noticed. He had made arrangements with the captain, and none of us were to be harmed. My dad looked at him. He handed him something. I'm not sure what it was. Woo looked at him, and a tear fell from his eyes. We were on our way."

"The voyage was long and difficult. The seas were rough. The temperatures reached unbearable levels. We were alone, several levels below the main deck. But there was always a helping hand. A shipmate would emerge and hand us some water. Another brought some rice. They all smiled and nodded. I felt we would be OK. My mom always held me tightly. I felt the security of family. My dad was there too. He was always within reach to comfort us when the seas swelled. They loved each other very much. Their feelings for each other and the comfort they gave me was a powerful lesson. I laid my head on her lap and snoozed off. It would be OK, it would be OK. We were family and would endure. They were my mentors. They taught me by example. There usually weren't too many words spoken. Just a certain look, just a certain gaze."

"I opened my eyes, and it was time to disembark. Woo had arranged for a pickup. We carried our bags to a worn-out 1950s Ford. Our driver's name was Chew. He threw our bags in. The old Ford belched and bucked but came to life. We climbed in. Woo had arranged for a drop-off point. The rest would be up to us."

"Lou, more of my story later. Where are we going?"

I didn't respond for a while. Swoosh, swoosh, swish, swish. The wipers continued their rhythm. I looked out the rain-beaded window and thought about where our lives were headed. Ralphie clearly had lots more to say.

25

"Ralph, pull off at Exit 30 in Newark." I was going to show him a good time. He deserved it.

"Ralph, make your second right. Ralph, make your next left. Ahh, there it is: the Pootsey Wooney Go-Go joint. The only doggie-only go-go operation on the East Coast."

His eyes opened wide. He gave me a wry little smile. This was going to be fun. The rain had subsided.

"Ralph, we need to make a proper entrance."

He opened my door. I stood up straight in the parking lot.

"Ralph, watch me."

I turned around and slowly started the skip—the one that Curly from the Three Stooges made famous. The move is more difficult than it looks. It's not exactly Olympic gymnastics, but you need to be balanced. Focus on your center of gravity. Lean forward slightly. Slightly bend the left knee. Place your right-foot toes on the ground. Kick up the right leg, keep going, get the rhythm, and keep going.

Ralphie got it! We reverse skipped through the parking lot in tandem. What fun we were having! Around and around we went. Practice makes perfect. Ralphs's hat was a little askew, but he had a big smile, and with his new shave and new suit, he was in heaven.

"Time to head in, Ralph."

"Oh yes," he said. "Let's go."

Our bonding continued. We were becoming companions, but who would be the mentor? It may not matter. Time would tell.

We entered through the slightly open door. We skipped in reverse, both in rhythm. The crowd applauded. Ralphie and I sat at a table for two. The house was full—shepherds, collies, even a golden retriever or two. A really cute poodle took the stage. She had a few extra years on her, but hubba hubba. All the right stuff was in the right places. Or so we thought. Even though her eight mammaries were enhanced, they looked great. We called her Two-Step. One step forward, one step back. She turned slowly. One step forward, one step back. Most girls used the pole, climbing up, sliding down. But not Two-Step. She had a bad hip, and her overpainted paws may have hindered her.

Ralphie was having a ball. He looked around, his eyes bulging. He had never seen anything like this. She came closer and smiled at Ralphie. Then her teeth fell out! Maybe this wasn't a great idea.

I handed Ralph a twenty.

Ralph donned his hat. With that, we reverse skipped out again. Once again the crowd stood and applauded. Goldens and poodles, shih tzos and labs, they all stood up. Thanks, it was time to hunker down.

"Where to, Chief?"
"Ralph, DON'T CALL ME CHIEF!"
"Sorry, Lou."

"Let's find somewhere to bed down. We can start fresh in the morning. Ahh, perfect. Motel 9. Just the two of us."

A couple blasts each, and we were off to sleep. Snoring and blasting, blasting and snoring. It was so much fun.

We woke early. Both of us had lots of crust in our eyes. We cleaned up, and Ralph loaded me in. It's tough for a little shih tzo. You know, get up, shower, put on the suit, and then drive the Loumobile.

But he could do it. He pulled the choke and stepped on the gas, and we were off. The weather had cleared up. I was dressed for success, and Ralph looked sharp.

"Where to, Lou?" Ralph asked.

"Ralph, just get me to the NY Expressway North. We are going to see an old friend."

"Sure, Chief."

"DON'T CALL ME CHIEF."

"You got it, Lou."

Off we went. The Loumobile accelerated perfectly. It had lots of power and a wonderful, SMOOTH ride. The shifting was perfect. The weather was perfect, cold and crisp. The sky was a deep blue, just like Ralph's eyes.

"Ralphie," I called, "how are you doing?"

"Fine, Lou, fine, Lou."

He put his sunglasses on. You know, the aviator type. They were a little oversized for his face, but he looked great.

We were on the road for an hour or so without much conversation—just Ralph in his world and me in mine. We were both in deep thought. Sometimes it's best to say nothing. Just be with yourself, with your own thoughts. We don't need to speak 24-7. Our society is obsessed with yapping. Call, text, email, and phone. My head could spin. Sometimes silence is golden. Quiet, peace and quiet. It can be cathartic. Not the worst thing.

It was getting chilly, so I turned up the heat a bit. That felt good. A little heat can be comforting, especially when it's fifteen degrees outside.

Ralph snapped out of his thoughts.

"Where are we going, Lou?"

"Turn off at Exit 55 in the Catskills."

We exited the throughway.

"Why, Lou? Who are we going to visit?"

"Eddy, Eddy P He is a wonderful friend of mine. Eddy is now disabled. But he was a champion wrestler, one of the best in the country. He wrestled for Lehigh University for two years. Wrestling is a demanding sport. The physical toll on your body could bring even the strongest man to his knees. But it's also a very demanding mental sport. Strategy and tactics. Sizing up your opponent. Split-second timing. There are only a few remaining from the class of 1953. We are going to pay our respects to him. Ed left college early. He decided that serving his country was more important than a diploma from a school."

Ralph shuddered a little bit. Something had disturbed him. But I didn't ask. We could talk later.

So up the road we went. This region of New York is known as the Catskills Mountain area. The mountains are large. Not quite Rocky Mountain in scale, but very impressive. They rose tens of thousands of years ago. The Ice Age glaciers had carved them into a work of art, partially frozen streams, wonderful scenic valleys, frozen ponds. Bare apple orchards everywhere. It must be gorgeous in the spring, I thought. I closed my eyes and envisioned. Just Lou and a fly-fishing pole. No one around. Just a beautiful stream and the hope of catching the perfect trout. I would return.

We turned and twisted, twisted and turned, through narrow valleys. Up we travelled, one thousand feet, two thousand feet, three thousand feet. It was exhilarating. Ralph handled the Loumobile with ease. He negotiated every turn and undulation expertly.

Then finally we arrived at Eddy's house. He lived with his wife in a beautiful log cabin. Eddy had developed a unique business. They supplied and constructed log cabins. He now resided in one of his own creations. Their home was situated at the top of a hill. The view was magnificent. His wife knew we were coming, but Eddy did not.

29

Ralphie opened the car door. I stepped out. We walked slowly to the front door. I wasn't sure what to expect. Knock knock.

His wife opened the door. Her name was Sarah. She had grown a little portly over the years but was dressed to the nines—pearls, with a beautiful skirt and top. She had protected herself with a terry cloth apron. Her eyes glistened. She thanked us for coming. It had been years, but she still had a spark.

Sarah invited us into her home. She spoke quietly.

"He doesn't know you are coming," she said.

"Eddy will be so pleased."

Ralph followed us in. He was very respectful of our reunion. Ralph took his hat off, bowed, and shook her hand. He stepped aside.

"What a polite young man," she whispered to me.

Even though Ralph could not reach her, she bent over and reached out to him. It was a simple kiss on the head.

Ralph blushed. Just a little dog, ten inches inches tall, he appreciated her act of kindness.

She asked us to follow her.

"Eddy, Eddy! I have a few visitors for lunch."

"Yuk," he groaned.

With that we walked into the kitchen area, a beautiful small room surrounded by glass. The view was wonderful. It overlooked the Bellaire Valley. We could see for miles and miles. The Berkshire Hills of Massachusetts were visible through the frosty light haze.

Eddy slowly turned his head. At this point he was confined to a wheelchair. He had developed Lou Gehrig's disease, which slowly shuts your body down. It's a disease that renders one helpless except for the mind. Eddy's jaw dropped, and his eyes filled with moisture.

"Lou, Lou, you SOB, come over here. After all this time has passed, you have returned. I am honored."

"The honor is mine," I said.

He smiled that great smile from many years ago.

"You look great! Not a day over a hundred!"

Eddy still had that wonderful, wry sense of humor.

"Please sit down, and your friend too."

I introduced Ralph. His wife stood in the corner and watched the reunion unfold.

Sarah brought out a little booster chair, and Ralph climbed up.

"Thank you," he said.

"And what do you do, Ralph?"

"I drive Lou in the Loumobile. It's a 1940 Caddy. You know, the godfather style. Lou and I are on a driving adventure! I drive, he rides."

Eddy looked at me with disbelief.

I nodded yes, that it was true.

Eddy laughed and laughed.

Sarah glanced over at us. She had not heard this laugh in years. Eddy left college after his sophomore year. He was committed to serve his country during the Korean War. He was not unique for the time. When our country called, they responded. He gave up a wonderful educational opportunity at a first-rate school. He also forfeited his wrestling scholarship, maybe even a chance at Olympic greatness.

Eddy volunteered for the paratroopers—not an easy assignment. It was very physical and dangerous. But that was his nature—never one to shy from a challenge.

Following the war he began his career. Eddy was always very artistic. He had a great knack for drawing. He also had an interest in log homes. He began to sketch some elevations. His business took off, and Eddy was on his way.

And now we sat across from each other. Time has taken its toll on both of us, but as usual, we enjoy each other's company.

Sara brought out some deviled eggs, chicken soup, and sandwiches. Nothing complicated. Just some nice comfort food, perfect for our reunion.

She sat and watched the reunion unfold. At times she would correct Eddy about a detail or two of his stories. Eddy and Sara met early in life. She was a beauty queen, he a handsome private about to enter the army. The story was from a romance book. He went AWOL and they eloped. The story even made the front page of the *NY Daily News*. They had been together ever since and were clearly still in love.

It started to snow. Just a light sparkly type, the kind that glistens as it falls. Without a lot of wind, the flakes performed a dance, very light and easy but beautiful to watch.

Eddy was clearly in some distress, but he still maintained that wonderful sense of humor. Ralph just listened and nodded, clearly enjoying how the happy reunion affected his new companion. He chuckled as the two old friends exchanged memories, even though Eddy was wheelchair bound and loved to sit near his fireplace.

Ralph jumped off his booster chair and maneuvered Eddy to his favorite spot. We talked some more, sharing stories about good, bad, and in-between times. Sara placed another soft blanket on Eddy.

He had a final story to tell.

"Lou, it's been wonderful to see you. I must share a story with you. One of individual heroics. One that saved my life. We were on a mission over North Korea and became disoriented. The navigational system had gone down. We were cruising along at fifteen thousand feet in a pea-soup-like fog. The jumpmaster ordered us to go."

Ralphie's eyes opened wide.

"Down we fluttered, zero visibility, to the ground. Total vertigo. We knew there was plenty of danger below. My M-1 was loaded and ready to go. We had drifted into China, somewhere along the Yangtze River. I crashed through a grove of pine trees and ended up suspended fifteen feet above the ground. I would have to cut myself loose. Thud! The ground was hard and rocky."

"I needed to locate a safe location. There was a flutter of noise in the distance. This could be the end of the road for ole Eddy boy. Stealth was the name of the game."

"Then he emerged. He quietly introduced himself. 'My name is Woo,' he whispered in broken English. 'You are an American friend. Follow me! I will lead you to safety.'"

Ralph shuddered, and a tear fell down his fuzzy cheek. Could Woo be Ralphie's Woo? Eddy had no idea of the significance of this story.

"Woo motioned me to follow him. We journeyed through the brush and thickets while dodging enemy forces."

Eddy explained that without Woo, he would not have survived. Eddy motioned toward the warmth of the fireplace and the view beyond. "Lou, I have had a long, enjoyable life. But I have learned through many circumstances that without friends, true friends like you, Woo, and many others, life would have been very shallow. I truly appreciate your visit. Thank you too, Ralph, take care of Lou. He is my mentor."

I moved closer to Eddy, put my arm around him, and whispered,

"No, Eddy, you are mine."

Ralphie hugged Eddy and donned his cap. We turned and without another spoken word bid our final good-bye. Before Ralphie opened the Loumobile door, I turned one more time toward Ed's home. I could see him through the window glass. Sara had stood Eddy up one last time. He stood ramrod straight and saluted us.

"Our reunion could have been sad and melancholy, but it was not. Acknowledge those mentors and true companions in your life. That's what our journey is all about, Ralphie."

With that, Ralphie loaded me in. Full choke, partial gas, boom boom, fart fart, two puffs of smoke, and the Loumobile belched to life. Ralphie smoothly shifted into first gear, and we slowly rolled away from Ed's log cabin.

The mist had resumed.

"Ralph! Wipers, please!"

"Sure Lou."

Swish, swish, swoosh, swoosh.

I settled back into my wonderful, deep, leather seat. It was time to relight my Johnny Appleseed pipe, close my eyes, and savor our reunion with Eddy. We began our reverse trip winding down the Catskill Valley.

"Ralphie, a little more heat, please. So what are your thoughts, Ralphie boy?" I could tell that the reunion meant a lot to him.

"He is a wonderful man, Lou. One we should all hope to be. So gentle and wise. Someone who has earned his stripes."

"So, Ralphie, where would YOU like to go?"

"Skiing!"

"Skiing!"

"And then I have a reunion too."

This should be fun, I thought.

The sun was setting, and the temperatures were dropping.

"Ralphie boy, let's begin fresh in the morning. Let's bunk at a real local motel. No Marriot for us. Find one near Bellaire Mountain."

Bellaire was a historical, old-school mountain resort. Developed in the 1940s, it was one of the oldest original ski areas on the East Coast. Not much vertical drop, but lots of fun. The mountain originally had just one rope tow, but the owners made modest improvements over the years. Chairlift and T-bars were added in the 1960s. A wonderful log-style lodge was nestled comfortably at the top of the mountain. It was unusual since most lodges are constructed at the resort base. I guess topography had a lot to do with the decision. We later found out that Eddy was instrumental in its design and construction.

I had been there before, and I knew that a huge Adirondack-style fireplace adorned the interior—a welcoming sight to the shivering skiers and guests. The sweet odor of hot chocolate always permeated the interior.

We were within striking distance of Bellaire.

"There, Ralphie! Pull into that spot. Perfect."

The Wagon Wheel Motel's nice, big, red neon VACANCY sign blinked in the night. Twenty-nine ninety-nine per night INCLUDING continental breakfast. What could be better?

We entered our room. It was a little cheesy, but I had been there before. The 1960s faux skier wallpaper was peeling, but what the heck. We climbed into our respective lumpy single beds and blew off a few beauties each.

"Night, Ralphie."

"Night, Lou. You are a great mentor, Lou."

"Thanks, Ralphie."

With that it was lights out, and we fell into a deep, snoring slumber—one that only guys can understand.

The sun peeked in through the torn window shade. The worn-out alarm sounded twice.

"Ralphie, Ralphie! Up and at 'em. It's time to ski!"

Now it was my turn to mentor once again.

It had snowed overnight, so we had to add chains to the tires. And once again, Ralphie fired up the Loumobile. Choke, some fuel, boom, and two puffs of smoke, and we were off to Bellaire.

I love the sound of chains on fresh snow. Cling, clang, with a little squeaky sound between the snow and the tires. A soothing rhythm, one that we don't hear much anymore.

We pulled into the parking lot. Fortunately, Bellaire had a dog ski and skate rental shop. Dogs were everywhere. Poodles, labs, shepherds, basset hounds, all scurrying to get to the slope first.

We outfitted Ralphie, and it was time for him to ski the mountain. I even bought him a new hat and goggles. He looked great. But then something distracted him. A hot French poodle in a tight, one-piece fur outfit wiggled out of the rental area.

"RALPHIE, HEY, there will be time for that later!"

Boys will be boys. We grabbed a hot chocolate and headed for the slopes. I strapped his skis on. He looked at me with some fear.

"Ralphie, let's go!"

With that he smiled that great smile, pulled his goggles down, and off we went. We were bombing down the slopes. Run after run he followed me, and then I followed him. Not bad for a beginner, I thought. His French-styled scarf was flying in the wind. We flew over some huge moguls, catching serious air. He turned his head once more. His smile was so big, there were icicles building up on his little fangs, sort of like ice on the pitot tube of an aircraft. The sun was setting, and the slope was icing up.

"RALPHIE, stop turning around. RAAALLPHIE!"

It was too late. He didn't see the tree. Smash, thud! The tree won.

"Ralphie, next time listen to your mentor."

We stumbled back to the lodge. Ralphie had earned a huge shiner, but sometimes misfortune pays dividends. The French Poodle, Fifi, greeted Ralphie.

"OHH, sit down, you poor thing."

With that, they sat fireside. She was whispering nothings into his floppy ear. He looked at me through the corner of his eye and winked.

I didn't see him till the next morning.

"Hey, buddy, how did it go?"

"Niccce," was all he could say.

We climbed in the Loumobile. Without a hitch the big V-8 kicked in.

"Ralph, ever fly an airplane?"

"Sure, Lou, it's something I've done every day. Duh. How many times have you seen a shih tzo fly an airplane?"

"Let's go flying, Ralphie."

"Oh YESSS," he said.

I relit my pipe and sat back.

"Ralph, take us to Woodstock. I know a great airfield there."

Ralph fit his aviator sunglasses to his face, and we were off—another opportunity to mentor my young companion.

I wanted to return to our conversation about Allentown. We had some time to travel.

"Tell me more about Allentown. Where did Chew drop you off? What happened next?"

There was a subtle shudder to his demeanor.

We entered the thruway. Ralph shifted the gears smoothly from first to fourth. The speedometer climbed to 75 mph. The morning was crisp, and some frost was on the windshield.

"Chew left us at a halfway house for illegal shih tzo families. We were guided through a dimly lit hall to a base-ment room. There were many other families crowded into a few rooms. My mom and dad thought about their decision. Was it the right thing to do? We were free, but free from what? Would our lives truly improve?"

"Days went by, then weeks. Nothing happened. The conditions seemed to worsen. My mom and dad encour-aged me. It would be OK. Once again I counted on their counsel and guidance."

"Something began to disturb me. Every other day or so, the landlord would come in and remove my mom. She would return late in the day looking disheveled and forlorn. My dad reached out, and she handed him a few dollars. Where did she go? What did she do? I wondered. At times youth has its benefits. In this case, naivety protected me from the reality of her situation."

I could see Ralph in the rearview mirror. I gently nodded. "Ralph, pull off here. It's time to fly!"

The airport was a throwback to simpler times: one grass landing strip, a few worn hangars, and some biplanes. I knew the owner and had told him we were coming. His name was Walt. Walt was a former World War II pilot who was willing to lend me his beautiful Waco biplane for an hour or so. I was also an expert flyer with many hours of experience.

There we were, in our beautiful 1940 Caddy, sitting next to the Waco.

Walt was all prepared for us.

"Come here, little fella." He decked Ralph out in scarf, leather jacket, and helmet.

"Slip these goggles on," he said.

We climbed in and took off. The engine had a low, powerful rumble. I pushed the throttle full forward. Higher and higher we climbed. This was an open-cockpit biplane. The engine and wind noise were intense, but it added to the excitement of the flight.

Ralph's hands were over his head. His little ears were sticking out from the leather helmet.

"FASTER, LOU, FASTER."

Round and round and round we went. It was joyous. Pure freedom. Ralph and I laughed and laughed and laughed. Ecstasy! No one could harm us up here! I was his mentor; we were companions. It was wonderful.

I set the big Waco down in a perfect three-point landing. We taxied over to Walt, and he threw a ladder up to Ralph.

"I feel like a fighter pilot returning home from a successful mission," Ralph said.

We thanked Walt for lending us his beautiful airplane. Ralph opened the door for me. We were about to conclude our journey.

5

TRAVELS: THE FINAL DAYS

farewell n 1: *a wish of welfare at parting :*
GOOD-BYE 2. LEAVE-TAKING

"Ralphie, let's head home."
"OK, Chief, whatever you say."
"DON'T CALL ME CHIEF!"
"Sorry, Lou."

Once again Ralph fired up the Loumobile. We waved to Walt. He appreciated our thumbs-up.

"Where to, Lou?"

"Let's go home."

Ralph pointed the long Loumobile nose south. I relit my pipe, poured a little tumbler of cognac, and we were off. Down the valley we went. The windshield was still coated with frost. I was thinking a lot about our journey. Ralphie had been totally devoted to my needs. He had been very respectful of me. He was becoming my mentor.

We pulled onto the thruway. Ralph shifted the Loumobile into fourth gear. AHH, nice and smooth. We continued south.

I'd like to repay him for his devotion to me, I thought.

We were cruising at a consistent 75 mph. Then I spotted the sign, a thirty-foot billboard: "Doggie Massage & Spa, All Dogs Welcome, Hot Tubs and Sauna Available!"

"Ralphie! Pull off at Exit 35. It's bonus time for you!"

"Sure, Lou."

He pulled off his sunglasses and parked the big Loumobile in the lot. The neon light blinked bright red: "Doggie Spa, Open 24 hours!"

We were greeted by the proprietor, Happie Hending. She welcomed us with grace and style.

"So, we have three levels of service: massage, massage and shower, and deluxe." She explained.

"Happie, this is my companion Ralphie. He deserves the best. Please take care of him. Deluxe service for Ralphie!"

Happie was a beautiful Shih tzo. I knew they would bond and she would service him well. She brought a little robe out for Ralphie. He undressed and followed her in. Within an hour he emerged. Ralph needed some sugar. He looked sooo relaxed.

"OJ, please!"

"How did it go, Ralph?"

He just stared at me, a little drool coming out of his mouth.

"Thanks, Lou."

That was it. TIME TO GO.

"Point her south, Ralph."

With that command, he fired up the Loumobile.

I lit my pipe once more and poured a tumbler of cognac.

"Ralphie, we have a few miles to go. Please continue with your story. No interruptions this time."

"Sure, Chief."
"DON'T CALL ME CHIEF!" I yelled.
"Sorry, Lou."

As we descended, the light snow turned to a misty rain. Once again the wipers came on. Just a slow swish, swish, whoosh, whoosh.

"With some help we were able to move from the boarding house to a small flat on the south side of Bethlehem, PA. There were two rooms. One was a kitchen/living room. The other was a bedroom we shared. One light bulb lit the kitchen. One overhead lit the bedroom. Just a simple stove, a small ice-box, a table, and a small couch adorned the living area. The icebox was just that: a small, insulated box. We filled it with ice every day to keep our food from spoiling. That was one of my jobs, Lou. But I felt gratified bringing home the big cube of ice knowing I was contributing to our family's well-being."

"We couldn't afford a TV, but one day dad brought home a radio. Now that he was employed at the local steel mill, we could afford a few 'luxuries.' "
"It was a simple, wonderful life. Once Dad returned home, we would sit and talk around the supper table. He would describe his day, never complaining but painting a picture of how difficult the work was at the mill. But he would ALWAYS turn the conversation to me.
'So, Ralphie, how was your day?' he would ask.
"'Great, Dad,' I would say. 'Mom is teaching me another language, Spanish.' Uch, but she said it would help me in the future. Times were going to change, she would say."

"After supper we would turn the radio on. There were programs of news, music, and stories. We would sit on our torn couch together and just listen. That's not something families do much anymore, just sit and listen together. It's all about who's wearing this, and who's doing that. Blah, blah, blah. But that's another story. One of my favorite shows was *The Jean Shepherd Show*. Dad would click on the radio, and Jean would just start to talk. It could be about anything: his dog, a bus ride, a favorite meal at a diner. He would go on and on. It wasn't scripted, just a free flow of his thoughts. It was so soothing to me, Lou. Halfway into one of his stories, I would lean over onto mom's or dad's lap. It was so calming to know they were there for me."

"And then I would wake up with sun shining through the torn shade. But it didn't matter. I was safe and looking forward to another day."

Ralphie turned the Loumobile west. We were on our final stretch. I relit my pipe.

"So go on, Ralphie."

"Mom taught me well. I was able to apply and get accepted to the local university. It was a renowned engineering and business school. Mom joined dad at the steel mill. I worked two part-time jobs to help with the tuition. But times were changing. The unions had negotiated pay levels that the mill couldn't afford. While it worked for a while, pressure from faraway lands was chipping away at our competitive status. It was just a matter of time."

I watched through my window as the rolling hills of western New Jersey passed by. What a beautiful region of the country, I thought. For such a small state, the geographical variety is truly amazing. There were mountains in the northwest, the Atlantic Ocean to the east. The access to New York City and Philadelphia was simple. The primitive Pine Barrens spread for endless miles in the south. The abundance of wildlife would amaze those unfamiliar with the Garden State. Black bear, deer, bald eagles, coyote and fox were in abundance.

New Jersey is actually a peninsula. She is bordered on the west by the beautiful Delaware River. The Delaware is actually two hundred-plus miles long and offers a tremendous variety of recreational activities. Fishing, canoeing, and kayaking are just a few. The northern end is dotted with many historic river towns—Frenchtown, Stockton, and Lambertville are just a few. These towns date back to the pre-revolutionary days. In fact, on a cold December day, General George Washington departed Lambertville and crossed the Delaware River. He guided his troops south and attacked the British in Trenton. The victory was enormous and dealt the Brits a terrible blow. The Atlantic Ocean borders the eastern side of this huge peninsula called New Jersey for 120 miles. This portion of the Atlantic offers some of the most productive fishing waters in the United States. Tuna, cod, shark, fluke, blue fish, and huge stripers abound. New Jersey is also the number-one producer of scallops in the world. Who would have thunk it? Let's keep that our secret. Let those folks from the remaining states think what they will.

Ralphie continued.

"Dad was laid off. Twenty years of hard labor and nothing to show for it. He began taking to the bottle. He tried many times but couldn't find a job. He drifted away. The last time I saw him, his head hung low. 'I'll be back,' he said.

"Mom was barely hanging on. My scholarship funds were going to run out this semester. Mom suggested I learn one more language before time ran out.

She said, 'Just pick something fun. Select one *for* pure enjoyment.'

"French it was. Oh yeah, just the sound was sexy. It could prove very useful for my future European travel plans."

I looked ahead; we were crossing the bridge over the Delaware and back into Pennsylvania. Hey, just like ole George, I thought.

"At the end of my final semester, my mom took ill and passed away quietly in her sleep. She was such a kind and simple woman. I shed tears for weeks. My mom was my true mentor, companion, and friend. I think of her everyday and the sacrifices she and my dad made for me. Her last wish was that someday I would finish my education.

Our landlord Elizabeth was a woman with a huge soul. But her financial situation was stressed. She could no longer care for me. Let me remind you Lou, my mom had schooled me. I was a very smart young man but only thirteen when accepted to the university. She did the best she could for me and just counted on someone like you to come through."

Ralph continued his employment with Lou for the next ten years. They lived together on his wonderful fifty-acre estate in rural Pennsylvania, and Lou housed Ralph and attended his graduation from engineering school.

Lou passed early in life. He was only forty-five years old.

Ralph continued on with many other travels. His French came in handy on his frequent trips to France. He even crossed paths with Fifi in Paris. "What a piece of..." he could hear Lou call from the heavens above.

"Farewell, Ralphie!"

"Farewell, Lou."

THE END
(OR MAYBE NOT)

Made in the USA
San Bernardino, CA
12 February 2016